Rose

meets Mr Wintergarten

Bob Graham

WALKER BOOKS
LONDON

The morning the Summers family moved into their
new house, they felt at home. Faith and Rose put up
their pictures. Baby Blossom watched.

Mr and Mrs Summers planted pansies, petunias, daisies
and geraniums. Their garden was a carpet of flowers.
All before the sun went down.

Every morning, from the roof of their house, the Summers watched the sun come up.

The sun never touched the house next door. Next door, everything bristled. Next door lived Mr Wintergarten.

There were stories in the street about Mr Wintergarten.

"He's mean,"
said Emily.

"And horrible,"
said Arthur.

"He's got a dog like a
wolf," said Naomi.

"And a saltwater
crocodile."

"They say he rides on his crocodile at night," said Emily.
"And GETS YA!" Arthur shrieked.
"I don't believe you," said Rose. "Anyway, don't
 frighten Blossom."

"My dad lost his football over there when he was a boy,"
said Emily. "You can just see it through the prickles,
old and flat as a pancake."

"No one ever goes in there," said Arthur, "in case
Mr Wintergarten eats them."

"If your ball ever goes over," said Naomi, "forget it."

And just then, Rose's ball went straight over
Mr Wintergarten's fence!

Rose went to tell her mum.
"Well, honeybunch," Mum said, "you can get your ball
back. Why don't you just go and *ask* him?"

"Because he eats kids," said Rose.
"We'll take him some hot cakes instead," said Mum.
"And maybe some flowers."

Mr Wintergarten's front gate had not been opened for years. Rose heaved and pushed. The gate groaned and squeaked. Then slowly it swung open.

Rose could see that there *was* a dog – big as a wolf!
"I can't see any crocodile," she said.
"I should hope not," replied Mum, and threw the dog a cake.

Rose knocked at Mr Wintergarten's door.

"Who the devil is that?" shouted a voice from inside.
"It's me," said Rose, and tiptoed in.

"What do *you* want?" said Mr Wintergarten.
"I'm Rose Summers from next door. I've come to
ask for my ball back." She twisted her fingers

in her handkerchief. "I've brought some flowers,
and hot fairy cakes from my mum."
Mr Wintergarten glared at her.

His dinner was cold, grey and uninviting, with bits of gristle floating in it and mosquitoes breeding on top. But Rose could see that he wasn't eating children.

"Please may I look for my ball?" she asked.
"No," growled Mr Wintergarten. "Clear off!"

But when Rose had gone, Mr Wintergarten slowly
pushed back his chair – and did something he
hadn't done in years…

Mr Wintergarten opened his curtains.

He sat on his front step in the sun. "No one has ever asked for their ball back," he said to himself. "Or brought fairy cakes."

He saw Rose's ball and thoughtfully pushed it with his toe.

Next he did some darting movements that made his coat-tails fly in the sun.

And then Mr Wintergarten kicked the ball...

right back over the fence!

"Good kick!" said Rose.
"Thank you," replied Mr Wintergarten.

"Would someone mind throwing back my slipper?" he added.

"I will," said Rose.
She threw his slipper high into the air.

"Catch, Mr Wintergarten!" Rose called.
And Mr Wintergarten caught it.

For Charlotte and her best friend, Kelly

First published 1992 by Walker Books Ltd
87 Vauxhall Walk, London SE11 5HJ

© 1992 Blackbird Design Pty Ltd

First printed 1992
Printed and bound in Hong Kong by
South China Printing Co. (1988) Ltd.

British Library Cataloguing in Publication Data
Graham, Bob
Rose meets Mr Wintergarten.
I. Title
823'.914 [J]
ISBN 0-7445-2115-7